When I Was Little
A Four-Year-Old's Memoir of Her Youth

by Jamie Lee Curtis
illustrated by Laura Cornell

HarperCollins*Publishers*

The author wishes to thank Phyllis, Joanna, Marilyn, Laura,
her family, and always, Chris

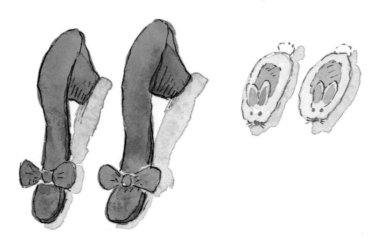

When I Was Little
A Four-Year-Old's Memoir of Her Youth
Text copyright © 1993 by Jamie Lee Curtis
Illustrations copyright © 1993 by Laura Cornell

Library of Congress Cataloging-in-Publication Data
Curtis, Jamie Lee, date
    When I was little: a four-year-old's memoir of her youth / by Jamie Lee Curtis; illustrated by
Laura Cornell.
    p.   cm.
    Summary: A four-year-old describes how she has changed since she was a baby.
    ISBN 0-06-021078-8. — ISBN 0-06-021079-6 (lib bdg.)
    ISBN 0-06-443423-0 (pbk.)
    [1. Babies—Fiction.   2. Growth—Fiction.]   I. Cornell, Laura, Ill.   II. Title.
PZ7.C948Wh   1993   91-46188
[E]—dc20   CIP
                                                                                      AC

Manufactured in China. All rights reserved.
For information address HarperCollins Children's Books,
a division of HarperCollins Publishers,
195 Broadway, New York, NY 10007.
17 18 19 20 SCP 40 39 38 37

For Annie
~J.L.C.

For Lilly
~L.C.

When I was little, I was a baby.

When I was little, I cried a lot.
Now I use words.

No

When I was little, I didn't know I was a girl.
My mom told me.

When I was little, I had silly hair. Now I can wear it in a ponytail or braids or pigtails or a pom-pom.

When I was little, I didn't get to eat
Captain Crunch or paint my toenails
bubble-gum pink.

CAP'N CRUNCH

Bubble-G Pink

The Big News

When I was little, I spilled a lot.
My mom said I was a handful.
Now I'm helpful.

When I was little, I rode in a baby car seat. Now I ride like a grown-up and wave at policemen.

When I was little, I went to Mommy and Me.

Now I go to nursery school and I have teachers and cubbies and naptime and secrets.

When I was little, I didn't understand
time-outs.
Now I do, but I don't like them.

When I was little, I made up words like
"scoopeeloo."
Now I make up songs.

When I was little, I swam in the pool with boys. I still do, but now we wear bathing suits but we don't wear floaties.

When I was little, the slide at the park was so big.

Now it's smaller, but I still like my granny to wait at the bottom for me.

When I was little, I ate goo and yucky stuff.

Now I eat pizza and noodles and fruit and Chee-tos.

When I was little, I had two teeth.
Now I have lots, and I know how to brush them.

When I was little, I slept in a zoo. Now I sleep in a big bed and get to play monkey.

When I was little, I kissed my mom and dad good night every night.
I still do, but only after they each read me a book and we play tickle torture.

When I was little, I didn't know what a family was.

When I was little, I didn't know what dreams were.

When I was little, I didn't know who I was.